• RHYME • TIME • READERS •

A Note to Parents

Rhyme, Repetition, and Reading are [illegible]n for your child. **Rhyme Time Readers** will introduce your child to the sounds of language, providing the foundation for reading success.

Rhyme

Children learn to listen and to speak before they learn to read. When you read this book, you are helping your child connect spoken language to written language. This increased awareness of sound helps your child with phonics and other important reading skills. While reading this book, encourage your child to identify the rhyming words on each page.

Repetition

Rhyme Time Readers have stories that your child will ask you to read over and over again. The words will become memorable due to frequent readings. To keep it fresh, take turns reading and encourage your child to chime in on the rhyming words.

Reading

Someday your child will be reading this book to you, as learning sounds leads to reading words and finally to reading stories like this one. I hope this book makes reading together a special experience.

Have fun and take the time
to let your child read and rhyme.

Francie Alexander
—Chief Education Officer,
Scholastic's Learning Ventures

To Mom and Jeff,
For always asking, no matter the answer—M.R.

For my own little pirate, Quinten.
With love, Grampy—G.U.

ISBN-13: 978-0-545-03412-8
ISBN-10: 0-545-03412-4

 Published by Scholastic Inc.
SCHOLASTIC, RHYME TIME READERS,
and associated logos are trademarks
and/or registered trademarks of Scholastic Inc.

12 11 10 9 8 7 6 5 4 3 2 1 7 8 9 10 11 12/0

Printed in the U.S.A.
First printing, September 2007

RHYME • TIME • READERS

Today at School

by Matt Ringler
Illustrated by George Ulrich

SCHOLASTIC INC.

New York Toronto London Auckland Sydney
Mexico City New Delhi Hong Kong Buenos Aires

I got off the bus and walked in the door.
I put my jacket away
and dropped my bag on the floor.

"Hey, Mom, it's me!"

Where could she be?

From the kitchen I heard her say,

"Did you have fun at school today?"

I thought for a while
then I gave her a smile.
Mom laughed. “Give me a clue.
What did you do?”

I said, “Nothing.”

“Nothing? Not one fun thing the entire day?
Didn’t Ms. Marina give you time to play?”

"I drove the trucks
and built with the blocks,
and we played with puppets
made out of socks."

Mom said, "That sounds like fun.
What else did you get done?"

I said, "Nothing."

"Nothing? Not one thing from the start?
Wasn't today your class's turn for art?"

“Yes,” I said. “I colored a dragon
shooting fire.
Ms. Marina hung it up for the class
to admire.”

Mom said, “Now *that* I want to see!
Anything else to tell me?”

I said, "Nothing."

"Nothing? Now I have a hunch,
that you must have done
something for lunch."

"Hank, Dan, and I sat in the back.
Before we ate, we each traded a snack."

Mom said, "Tomorrow I will pack you two,
one to trade and one for you."

Mom looked at me like she knew what
I would say,
but still she asked, "Did you do anything
else today?"

And that's when I said—

“I watched the class fish swim,

and I swung like a monkey on the jungle gym.

“We ran in a race
and I came in first place.

“Our teacher read us a book that was funny.
It was about a squirrel and a bunny.”

Mom was pleased. *What more would I say?*
"Sounds like you had quite a day!"

She said, "Tomorrow is school, too.
Any idea of what you will do?"

And I said, "Something."